To my mum, Maureen Harvey,
with lots of love D.H.

To all my family,
with much love L.R.

ORCHARD BOOKS
338 Euston Road, London NW1 3BH
*Orchard Books Australia*
Hachette Children's Books
Level 17/207 Kent Street, Sydney, NSW 2000

First published in 2007 by Orchard Books
Text © Damian Harvey 2007
Illustrations © Lucy Richards 2007

The rights of Damian Harvey to be identified as the author and
Lucy Richards to be identified as the illustrator of this work have been asserted
by them in accordance with the Copyright, Designs and Patents Act, 1988.

A CIP catalogue record for this book is available from the British Library.

ISBN: 978 1 84362 865 1

1 3 5 7 9 10 8 6 4 2

Printed in Singapore

Orchard Books is a division of Hachette Children's Books

# SNAP

## Damian Harvey
## Illustrated by Lucy Richards

ORCHARD BOOKS

Walking by the river one day,

Mother Duck found a little, lost egg.

So as quick as a quack, she rolled the
egg home and sat down

# plop!

on her nest.

She didn't have long to wait, before . . .

Crick!

Crack!

Crick!

. . . out popped one, two, three little ducklings – all fluffy and bright. Mother Duck named them Quack, Dabble and Fluff.

She looked sadly at the last egg and just when she thought it would never hatch . . .

crick! crack!

Crock! . . . it did!

Out popped **Something**
all wrinkly and **green**.

"What a tail!"
said Quack.

"What a beak!"
said Dabble.

"What is it?" said Fluff.

"He's your little brother,"
said Mother Duck.
"Now say hello."

"Hello," said Quack, Dabble and Fluff.
But all the wrinkly, green Something
said was, "Snap!"
So that's what Mother Duck named him.

Creatures came from near and far
to watch the ducklings' first swim.
Everyone said they were a sight to see,
each as lovely as the next, but...

"Look at the green one!" said Giraffe.

"He's all wrinkly!" giggled Monkey.

"And he's swimming underwater!" laughed Hippo.

"Some ducklings *are* different," quacked Mother Duck, "but to me, they're **all** wonderful."

Days and weeks passed, and Quack,
Dabble and Fluff grew **bigger** and **bigger**.

They lost their fluffy baby feathers and
grew beautiful new ones.

Snap grew too.

He got **bigger** and **stronger,**

and **faster** and **longer.**

But the other creatures still gossiped about Snap...

"Look at those big, staring eyes," they said.

"And that swishy-swash tail," they whispered.

"And that snippy-snap mouth," they gulped.

"Some ducklings *are* different," quacked Mother Duck, "but to me, they're **all** wonderful."

Then, one day, a hungry tiger
slunk down to the river...

He **sniffed** the air
and **licked** his lips...

"I smell **ducklings**," said Tiger.
"Plump and juicy and ready for eating."

Mother Duck huddled her children down in the reeds. And they didn't make a sound.

But Tiger padded closer, sniffing and snuffling until . . .

"Found you!"

roared Tiger.
"Now who shall
I gobble up first?"

"My little ones are too small to make a meal for you," cried Mother Duck. "Eat me instead!"

"But you are old and stringy," snorted Tiger, "and they are plump and tasty."

Tiger splish-splashed into the water.

Mother Duck, Quack, Dabble and Fluff
tried to scare Tiger away.

They **flapped**
their wings,

and **quacked**
their quacks.

But Tiger just **laughed** his laugh.

Suddenly, with a bubbling **splash**,
Snap leapt out of the water!
His big, round eyes stared,
his swishy-swash tail swished,
and his snippy-snap mouth

# SNAPPED

right on the
end of Tiger's nose!

Tiger howled and roared off into the jungle . . .

Quack, Dabble and Fluff clapped and flapped their wings in delight.